Button Time

Chapters

The Button Shop 2

Cityville 6

More Buttons 14

by Anne O'Brien
illustrated by Gil Ashby

Harcourt

Orlando   Boston   Dallas   Chicago   San Diego

Visit *The Learning Site!*

www.harcourtschool.com

The Button Shop

Hi! My name is Amanda. I want to tell you about an adventure that might never have happened if my brother, Zeke, hadn't lost a button from his jacket. Mom, Dad, Zeke, and I were on vacation in South Dakota. It was supposed to be a chance for my dad, the overworked writer, to take a break. Instead, he had to spend most of his time doing research for a book that he was writing about the old West.

Mom is a history professor. Naturally, she was happy to spend spring break poking around museums and libraries. Zeke and I were glad just to see a different part of the country for a few days. On that particular day, we made a stop in Sioux Falls.

We were walking down a side street when Mom saw a button shop.

"Look, everyone," she said, "maybe we can find a match for Zeke's jacket button." We all herded through the door and found ourselves in a dark little shop that looked as if it belonged in another time.

Some wooden signs with fancy old-fashioned writing hung on the walls. On some shelves behind the counter, there was a display of dolls made of cornhusks. In a corner a pioneer woman's dress hung on a dressmaker's form. There were buttons everywhere.

Mom, the history professor, and Dad, the writer, already had that look in their eyes. They'd found a hidden treasure. The place did not interest Zeke or me. After all, who cared about buttons? It was fun to see Mom and Dad so interested, though.

Then we heard a voice, sounding a little creaky, from the dim back corner of the shop.

"May I help you?" The voice belonged to an old man, tall and thin, with a short, pointed beard and round wire glasses. Mom held up Zeke's jacket to show the man the kind of button we needed. Zeke and I decided to look around the shop.

We found something that did interest us.
In the back of the shop, a wooden cabinet had a
handwritten sign that said "Antique Shell
Buttons—Conch and Pearl." The buttons were in
a small open display case. Below the case, a sign
said "DO NOT TOUCH." Now, what is it about
those words that just makes you itch to disobey
them? Anyway, they were just buttons. What
harm could be done?

Zeke and I both reached out. We each
touched a button with an index finger. There
was a sudden flash of light in the dark shop. I
closed my eyes and opened them to bright sun.

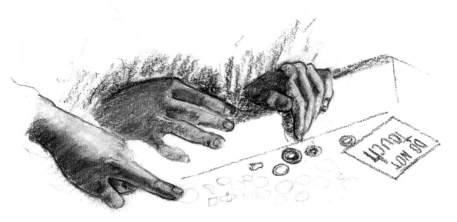

Cityville

The very first thing I noticed, with intense relief, was that we were all there. Mom, Dad, Zeke, and I were still together. Everything else around us had changed, though. First of all, I saw that we were outside. We were in a wide open space, with a huge treeless plain stretching out forever in front of us. There was nothing but grass, all the way to the horizon. It was quiet, except for an occasional rustle of grass. All the city sounds we'd been hearing had vanished.

Then a horse whinnied, and we all whirled around. We were surprised to see a strange town behind us. Well, I guess you could call it a town.

The town, or whatever it was, was only one block long. Both sides of the street had no more than twenty buildings, all made of wood. They were the kind you see in old cowboy movies. Some horses grazed in a paddock behind one of the buildings. We were at one end, where the town met the prairie. At the other end of the block, you could see a line of trees that served as a windbreak before the prairie began again.

We finally recovered enough to find our voices and all started talking at once.
No matter how we looked at it, no matter how impossible it was, we seemed to have traveled back in time.

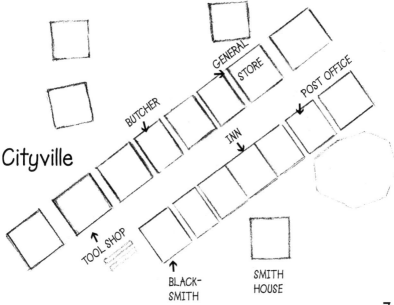

Cityville

GENERAL STORE

POST OFFICE

BUTCHER

INN

TOOL SHOP

BLACK-SMITH

SMITH HOUSE

We were alarmed, to say the least, and it took us a while to calm down. We realized we had to do something. We agreed to walk into the town, small as it was. At least the four of us were together.

The second building on the left had a big sign with old-fashioned writing that said "Cityville Post Office." We pushed open the door and walked in. Behind the counter was an old man, tall and thin, with a short, pointed beard and round wire glasses. I couldn't place him, but he looked kind of familiar.

He looked us up and down silently for a moment. Then he said, "You're not from around here, are you?"

We shook our heads.

"How long are you planning to stay?" he asked.

We all looked at Dad. He shrugged to give himself time to think of an answer. Then he drawled back, "Not sure yet." The old man looked us up and down again, measuring us.

"I've got a proposition for you," he said. "I'm heading off to California to look for gold. I've got folks waiting for me down the trail. The man coming to take my place here at the post office got delayed two weeks. It looks as though you could use a place to stay. If you run the post office until he gets here, you can stay upstairs."

That's how we ended up running the post office in Cityville, South Dakota, in 1849. Mom found the date on a calendar upstairs. She and Dad were excited about this new adventure. It took them a while to learn how things were mailed back then. People had to bring their letters to the post office to be mailed. Everyone also had to pick up his or her mail at the post office. There was no home delivery in a small town back then. Mom and Dad soon got used to their new job, though.

Zeke and I caught on pretty quickly that this wasn't going to be a vacation. Before he left, the old man showed us the food in the cupboards. All I saw was a lot of cans and sacks of stuff. He pointed to the wood stove we would use for heat and cooking. We would have to keep it going all the time to keep the building warm. We would use oil lamps for light, since there was no electricity back then. Outside, he showed us the pump where we would get water. Pumping that handle up and down sure made my arms sore.

By the third day, even Mom and Dad's excitement was wearing a little thin. Life in the old West was A LOT OF WORK!

First thing in the morning, we had to throw
wood in the stove. Even spring on the prairie
is still chilly. Then we had to cook some
breakfast, and I mean cook. There was no
pancake mix, no store-bought bread, and no
boxes of cereal. There were no frozen dinners,
either! We had to make everything from scratch.
There was also no supermarket to run to when
we ran out of supplies.

We had a lot of trouble at first. Keeping the
stove going and figuring out how to cook on it
were not easy. We ate some things that were
nearly burnt. We ate others that needed a lot
more cooking. The first week we dragged
around dead tired from all the work.

After breakfast, while Mom went downstairs to run the post office, Zeke and I would heat water to wash the dishes and do laundry. Dad chopped and split wood so we could keep the stove going. It went on like this all day, every day.

We found some clothes in a wardrobe. They didn't fit us perfectly, but they were good enough. Since Mom's and my hair is long, we looked like everyone else once we were dressed right. People seemed pretty used to strangers coming through on their way somewhere else. We let it be known that we were city folk. That gave people an explanation for anything strange we did.

We tried not to say much. We didn't want to tell anyone that we really came from more than 150 years in the future! Who would ever believe us? Of course, the bigger question was how would we ever get back there?

By the end of the second week, we began to get more comfortable in Cityville. Doing chores didn't tire me out as much. We got used to having no TV, no radio, no computer, and no video games. At night we played cards, sang songs, read to each other from the few books the old man had, and talked a lot. If we were stuck here, maybe living in the old West wouldn't be so bad, after all.

Of course, our minds changed again when Zeke found the peddler and his wagon. One minute he was outside, playing with some boys he'd met. Next thing we knew, he came bursting through the door, shouting, "Buttons! Buttons!" When he'd calmed down, he told us what he was so excited about. He had overheard some women saying that a peddler's wagon had come to town. The peddler was selling fabric, sewing supplies, pots and pans, and BUTTONS!

Mom packed up our own modern clothes in a cloth bundle. With our hearts beating furiously, we all hurried down to look at the wagon.

We gathered around the wagon, trying to act casual. We didn't want to look too thrilled about some silly buttons. We nodded politely to our neighbors.

"What lovely buttons you have. May I see a box of them?" Mom asked. We all held our breath. We might be going home before we knew it. The peddler showed us a box of buttons.

There, sure enough, were shell buttons that looked exactly like the antique ones in the button shop. Mom glanced at us, and Dad grabbed my hand. I grabbed Zeke's hand, and Zeke took Mom's hand, just in case. Then Mom reached down and touched one of the shell buttons.

15

FLASH! There we were, back in the button shop. Mom was holding the shell button now. The old man with the wire glasses was sitting there behind the counter smiling at us. He was happy to return the shell button to his collection of antiques.

By the way, Dad's book about life in the old West is selling really well. Everyone wonders how he managed to put in so many details about daily life. It makes readers think he must have lived in the old West himself. (Imagine that!) The success of the book has even given us a chance to take another vacation. This time, though, we're staying in this century.